A Thorny

Volume 08

Georg Ebers

(Translator: Clara Bell)

Alpha Editions

This edition published in 2023

ISBN : 9789357946599

Design and Setting By
Alpha Editions
www.alphaedis.com
Email - info@alphaedis.com

Contents

VOLUME 8.

CHAPTER XXIII.

The slave Argutis was waiting for Melissa in the antechamber. It was evident that he brought good news, for he beamed with joy as she came toward him; and before she left the house she knew that her father and Philip had returned and had regained their freedom.

The slave had not allowed these joyful tidings to reach his beloved mistress's ear, that he might have the undivided pleasure of bringing them himself, and the delight she expressed was fully as great as he had anticipated. Melissa even hurried back to Johanna to impart to her the joyful intelligence that she might tell it to her mistress.

When they were in the street the slave told her that, at break of day, the ship had cast anchor which brought back father and son. The prisoners had received their freedom while they were still at sea, and had been permitted to return home at once. All was well, only—he added, hesitatingly and with tears in his eyes—things were not as they used to be, and now the old were stronger than the young. Her father had taken no harm from the heavy work at the oars, but Philip had returned from the galleys very ill, and they had carried him forthwith to the bedchamber, where Dido was now nursing him. It was a good thing that she had not been there to hear how the master had stormed and cursed over the infamy they had had to endure; but the meeting with his birds had calmed him down quickly enough.

Melissa and her attendant were walking in the direction of the Serapeum, but now she declared that she must first see the liberated prisoners. And she insisted upon it, although Argutis assured her of her father's intention of seeking her at the house of the high-priest, as soon as he had removed all traces of his captivity and his shameful work at the galleys in the bath. Philip she would, of course, find at home, he being too weak to leave the house. The old man had some difficulty in following his young mistress, and she soon stepped lightly over the "Welcome" on the threshold of her father's house. Never had the red mosaic inscription seemed to shine so bright and friendly, and she heard her name called in delighted tones from the kitchen.

This joyful greeting from Dido was not to be returned from the door only. In a moment Melissa was standing by the hearth; but the slave, speechless with happiness, could only point with fork and spoon, first to the pot in which a large piece of meat was being boiled down into a strengthening soup for Philip, then to a spit on which two young chickens were browning before the fire, and then to the pan where she was frying the little fish of which the returned wanderer was so fond.

But the old woman's struggle between the duty that kept her near the fire and the love that drew her away from it was not of long duration. In a few minutes Melissa, her hands clasping the slave's withered arm, was listening to the tender words of welcome that Dido had ready for her. The slave woman declared that she scarcely dared to let her eyes rest upon her mistress, much less touch her with the fingers that had just been cleaning fish; for the girl was dressed as grandly as the daughter of the high-priest. Melissa laughed at this; but the slave went on to say that they had not been able to detain her master. His longing to see his daughter and the desire to speak with Caesar had driven him out of the house, and Alexander had, of course, accompanied him. Only Philip, poor, crushed worm, was at home, and the sight of her would put more strength into him than the strong soup and the old wine which his father had fetched for him from the store-room, although he generally reserved it for libations on her mother's grave.

Melissa soon stood beside her brother's couch, and the sight of him cast a dark shadow over the brightness of this happy morn. As he recognized her, a fleeting smile crossed the pale, spiritualized face, which seemed to her to have grown ten years older in this short time; but it vanished as quickly as it had come. Then the great eyes gazed blankly again from the shadows that surrounded them, and a spasm of pain quivered from time to time round the thin, tightly closed lips. Melissa could hardly restrain her tears. Was this what he had been brought to-the youth who only a few days ago had made them all feel conscious of the superiority of his brilliant mind!

Her warm heart made her feel more lovingly toward her sick brother than she had ever done when he was in health, and surely he was conscious of the tenderness with which she strove to comfort him.

The unaccustomed, hard, and degrading work at the oars, she assured him, would have worn out a stronger man than he; but he would soon be able to visit the Museum again and argue as bravely as ever. With this, she bent over him to kiss his brow, but he raised himself a little, and said, with a contemptuous smile:

"Apathy—ataraxy—complete indifference—is the highest aim after which the soul of the skeptic strives. That at least "=-and here his eyes flashed for a moment—"I have attained to in these cursed days. That a thinking being could become so utterly callous to everything—everything, be it what it may—even I could never have believed!" He sank into silence, but his sister urged him to take courage—surely many a glad day was before him yet.

At this he raised himself more energetically, and exclaimed:

"Glad days?—for me, and with you? That you should still be of such good cheer would please or else astonish me if I were still capable of those sentiments. If things were different, I should ask you now, what have you given the imperial bloodhound in return for our freedom?"

Here Melissa exclaimed indignantly, but he continued unabashed:

"Alexander says you have found favor with our imperial master. He calls, and you come. Naturally, it is for him to command. See how much can be made of the child of a gem-cutter! But what says handsome Diodoros to all this?— Why turn so pale? These, truly, are questions which I would fling in your face were things as they used to be. Now I say in all unconcern, do what you will!"

The blood had ebbed from Melissa's cheeks during this attack of her brother's. His injurious and false accusations roused her indignation to the utmost, but one glance at his weary, suffering face showed her how great was the pain he endured, and in her compassionate heart pity strove against righteous anger. The struggle was sharp, but pity prevailed; and, instead of punishing him by a sharp retort, she forced herself to explain to him in a few gentle words what had happened, in order to dispel the unworthy suspicion that must surely hurt him as much as it did her. She felt convinced that the sufferer would be cheered by her words; but he made no attempt to show that he appreciated her kindly moderation, nor to express any satisfaction. On the contrary, when he spoke it was in the same tone as before.

"If that be the case," he said, "so much the better; but were it otherwise, it would have to be endured just the same. I can think of nothing that could affect me now, and it is well. Only my body troubles me still. It weighs upon me like lead, and grows heavier with every word I utter. Therefore, I pray you, leave me to myself!"

But his sister would not obey. "No, Philip," she cried, eagerly, "this may not be. Let your strong spirit arise and burst asunder the bonds that fetter and cripple it."

At this a groan of pain escaped the philosopher, and, turning again to the girl, he answered, with a mournful smile:

"Bid the cushion in that arm-chair do so. It will succeed better than I!" Then crying out impatiently and as loudly as he could, "Now go—you know not how you torture me!" he turned away from her and buried his face in the pillows.

But Melissa, as if beside herself, laid her hands upon his shoulder, and, shaking him gently, exclaimed: "And even if it vexes you, I will not be driven away thus. The misfortunes that have befallen you in these days will end by destroying you, if you will not pull yourself together. We must have patience, and it can only come about slowly, but you must make an effort. The least thing that pains you hurts us too, and you, in return, may not remain indifferent to what we feel. See, Philip, our mother and Andrew taught us often not to think only of ourselves, but of others. We ask so little of you; but if you—"

At this the philosopher shook himself free of her hand, and cried in a voice of anguish:

"Away, I say! Leave me alone! One word more, and I die!" With this he hid his head in the coverlet, and Melissa could see how his limbs quivered convulsively as if shaken by an ague.

To see a being so dear to her thus utterly broken down cut her to the heart. Oh, that she could help him! If she did not succeed, or if he never found strength to rouse himself, he, too, would be one of Caesar's victims. Corrupted and ruined lives marked the path of this terrible being, and, with a shudder, she asked herself when her turn would come.

Her hair had become disordered, and as she smoothed it she looked in the mirror, and could not but observe that in the simple but costly white robe of the dead Korinna she looked like a maiden of noble birth rather than the lowly daughter of an artist. She would have liked to tear it off and replace it by another, but her one modest festival robe had been left behind at the house of the lady Berenike. To appear in broad daylight before the neighbors or to walk in the streets clad in this fashion seemed to her impossible after her brother's unjust suspicion, and she bade Argutis fetch her a litter.

When they parted, Dido could see distinctly that Philip had wounded her. And she could guess how, so she withheld any questions, that she might not hurt her. Over the fire, however, she stabbed fiercely into the fowl destined for the philosopher, but cooked it, nevertheless, with all possible care.

On the way to the Serapeum, Melissa's anxiety increased. Till now, eagerness for the fray, fear, hope, and the joyful consciousness of right-doing, had alternated in her mind. Now, for the first time, she was seized with a premonition of misfortune. Fate itself had turned against her. Even should she succeed in escaping, she could not hope to regain her lost peace of mind.

Philip's biting words had shown her what most of them must think of her; and, though the ship should bear her far away, would it be right to bring Diodoros away from his old father to follow her? She must see her lover, and if possible tell him all. The rose, too, which the Christian had given her for him, and which lay in her lap, she wished so much to carry to him herself. She could not go alone to the chamber of the convalescent, and the attendance of a slave counted for nothing in the eyes of other people. It was even doubtful if a bondsman might be admitted into the inner apartments of the sanctuary. However, she would, she must see Diodoros and speak to him; and thus planning ways and means by which to accomplish this, looking forward joyfully to the meeting with her father, and wondering how Agatha, the Christian, had received Alexander, she lost the feeling of deep depression which had weighed on her when she had left the house.

The litter stopped, and Argutis helped her to descend. He was breathless, for it had been most difficult to open a way for her through the dense crowds that were already thronging to the Circus, where the grand evening performance in honor of the emperor was to begin as soon as it was dark. Just as she was entering the house, she perceived Andreas coming toward them along the street of Hermes, and she at once bade the slave call him. He was soon at her side, and declared himself willing to accompany her to Diodoros.

This time, however, she did not find her lover alone in the sick-room. Two physicians were with him, and she grew pale as she recognized in one of them the emperor's Roman body-physician.

But it was too late too escape detection; so she only hastened to her lover's side, whispered warm words of love in his ear, and, while she gave him the rose, conjured him ever and always to have faith in her and in her love, whatever reports he might hear.

Diodoros was up and had fully recovered. His face lighted up with joy as he saw her; but, when she repeated the old, disquieting request, he anxiously begged to know what she meant by it. She assured him, however, that she had already delayed too long, and referred him to Andreas and the lady Euryale, who would relate to him what had befallen her and spoiled every happy hour she had. Then, thinking herself unobserved by those present, she breathed a kiss upon his lips. But he would not let her go, urging with passionate tenderness his rights as her betrothed, till she tore herself away from him and hurried from the room.

As she left, she heard a ringing laugh, followed by loud, sprightly talking. It was not her lover's voice, and endeavoring, while she waited for Andreas, to catch what was being said on the other side of the door, she distinctly heard the body-physician (for no other pronounced the Greek language in that curious, halting manner) exclaim, gayly: "By Cerberus, young man, you are to be envied! The beauty my sovereign lord is limping after flies unbidden into your arms!"

Then came loud laughter as before, but this time interrupted by Diodoros's indignant question as to what this all meant. At last Melissa heard Andreas's deep voice promising the young man to tell him everything later on; and when the convalescent impatiently asked for an immediate explanation, the Christian exhorted him to be calm, and finally requested the physician to grant him a few moments' conversation.

Then there was quiet for a time in the room, only broken by Diodoros's angry questions and the pacifying exclamations of the freedman. She felt as if she must return to her lover and tell him herself what she had been forced to do in these last days, but maidenly shyness restrained her, till at last Andreas came out. The freedman's honest face expressed the deepest solicitude, and his voice sounded rough and hasty as he exclaimed, "You must fly—fly this day!" And my father and brother, and Diodoros?" she asked, anxiously. But he answered, urgently:

"Let them get away as they may. There is no hole or corner obscure enough to keep you hidden. Therefore take advantage of the ship that waits for you. Follow Argutis at once to the lady Berenike. I can not accompany you, for it lies with me to occupy for the next few hours the attention of the body-physician, from whom you have the most to fear. He has consented to go with me to my garden across the water. There I promised him a delicious, real Alexandrian feast, and you know how gladly Polybius will seize the opportunity to share it with him. No doubt, too, some golden means may be found to bind his tongue; for woe to you if Caracalla discovers prematurely that you are promised to another, and woe then to your betrothed! After sundown, when every one here has gone to the Circus, I will take Diodoros to a place of safety. Farewell, child, and may our heavenly Father defend you!"

He laid his right hand upon her head as if in blessing; but Melissa cried, wringing her hands: "Oh, let me go to him once more! How can I leave him and go far away without one word of farewell or of forgiveness?"

But Andreas interrupted her, saying: "You can not. His life is at stake as well as your own. I shall make it my business to look after his safety. The wife of Seleukus will assist you in your flight."

"And you will persuade him to trust me?" urged Melissa, clinging convulsively to his arm.

"I will try," answered the freedman, gloomily. Melissa, dropped his arm, for loud, manly voices were approaching down the stairs near which they stood.

It was Heron and Alexander, returning from their audience with the emperor. Instantly the Christian went to meet them, and dismissed the temple servant who accompanied them.

In the half-darkness of the corridor, Melissa threw herself weeping into her father's arms. But he stroked her hair lovingly, and kissed her more tenderly on brow and eyes than he had ever clone before, whispering gayly to her: "Dry your tears, my darling. You have been a brave maiden, and now comes your reward. Fear and sorrow will now be changed into happiness and power, and all the glories of the world. I have not even told Alexander yet what promises to make our fortunes, for I know my duty." Then, raising his voice, he said to the freedman, "If I have been rightly informed, we shall find the son of Polybius in one of the apartments close at hand."

"Quite right," answered the freedman, gravely, and then went on to explain to the gem-cutter that he could not see Diodoros just now, but must instantly leave the country with his son and daughter on Berenike's ship. Not a moment was to be lost. Melissa would tell him all on the way.

But Heron laughed scornfully: "That would be a pretty business! We have plenty of time, and, with the greatness that lies before us, everything must be done openly and in the right way. My first thought, you see, was to come here, for I had promised the girl to Diodoros, and he must be informed before I can consent to her betrothal to another."

"Father!" cried Melissa, scarcely able to command her voice. But Heron took no notice of her, and continued, composedly: "Diodoros would have been dear to me as a son-in-law. I shall certainly tell him so. But when Caesar, the ruler of the world, condescends to ask a plain man for his daughter, every other consideration must naturally be put aside. Diodoros is sensible, and is sure to see it in the right light. We all know how Caesar treats those who are in his way; but I wish the son of Polybius no ill, so I forbore to betray to Caesar what tie had once bound you, my child, to the gallant youth."

Heron had never liked the freedman. The man's firm character had always gone against the gemcutter's surly, capricious nature; and it was no little satisfaction to him to let him feel his superiority, and boast before him of the apparent good luck that had befallen the artist's family.

But Andreas had already heard from the physician that Caracalla had informed his mother's envoys of his intended marriage with an Alexandrian, the daughter of an artist of Macedonian extraction. This could only refer to Melissa, and it was this news which had caused him to urge the maiden to instant flight.

Pale, incapable of uttering a word, Melissa stood before her father; but the freedman grasped her hand, looked Heron reproachfully in the face, and asked, quietly, "And you would really have the heart to join this dear child's life to that of a bloody tyrant?"

"Certainly I have," returned Heron with decision, and he drew his daughter's hand out of that of Andreas, who turned his back upon the artist with a meaning shrug of the shoulders. But Melissa ran after him, and, clinging to him, cried as she turned first to him and then to her father:

"I am promised to Diodoros, and shall hold fast to him and my love; tell him that, Andreas! Come what may, I will be his and his alone! Caesar—"

"Swear not!" broke in Heron, angrily, "for by great Serapis—"

But Alexander interposed between them, and begged his father to consider what he was asking of the girl. Caesar's proposals could scarcely have been very pleasing to him, or why had he concealed till now what Caracalla was whispering to him in the adjoining room? He might imagine for himself what fate awaited the helpless child at the side of a husband at whose name even men trembled. He should remember her mother, and what she would have said to such a union. There was little, time to escape from this terrible wooer.

Then Melissa turned to her brother and begged him earnestly: "Then you take me to the ship Alexander; take charge of me yourself!"

"And I?" asked Heron, his eye cast gloomily on the ground.

"You must come with us!" implored the girl, clasping her hands.—"O Andreas! say something! Tell him what I have to expect!"

"He knows that without my telling him," replied the freedman. "I must go now, for two lives are at stake, Heron. If I can not keep the physician away from Caesar, your daughter, too, will be in danger. If you desire to see your daughter forever in fear of death, give her in marriage to Caracalla. If you have her happiness at heart, then escape with her into a far country."

He nodded to the brother and sister, and returned to the sick-room.

"Fly!—escape!" repeated the old man, and he waived his hand angrily. "This Andreas—the freedman, the Christian—always in extremes. Why run one's head against the wall? First consider, then act; that was what she taught us whose sacred memory you have but now invoked, Alexander."

With this he walked out of the half-dark corridor into the open court- yard, in front of his children. Here he looked at his daughter, who was breathing fast, and evidently prepared to resist to the last. And as he beheld her in Korinna's white and costly robes, like a noble priestess, it occurred to him that even before his captivity she had ceased to be the humble, unquestioning instrument of his capricious temper. Into what a haughty beauty the quiet embroideress had been transformed!

By all the gods! Caracalla had no cause to be ashamed of such an empress.

And, unaccustomed as he was to keep back anything whatever from his children, he began to express these sentiments. But he did not get far, for the hour for the morning meal being just over, the court-yard began to fill from all sides with officials and servants of the temple. So, father and son silently followed the maiden through the crowded galleries and apartments, into the house of the highpriest.

Here they were received by Philostratus, who hardly gave Melissa time to greet the lady Euryale before he informed her, but with unwonted hurry and excitement, that the emperor was awaiting her with impatience.

The philosopher motioned to her to follow him, but she clung, as if seeking help, to her brother, and cried: "I will not go again to Caracalla! You are the kindest and best of them all, Philostratus, and you will understand me. Evil will come of it if I follow you—I can not go again to Caesar."

But it was impossible for the courtier to yield to her, in the face of his monarch's direct commands; therefore, hard as it was to him, he said, resolutely: "I well understand what holds you back; still, if you would not ruin yourself and your family, you must submit. Besides which, you know not what Caesar is about to offer you-fortunate, unhappy child!"

"I know—oh, I know it!" sobbed Melissa; "but it is just that . . . I have served the emperor willingly, but before I consent become the wife of such a monster—"

"She is right," broke in Euryale, and drew Melissa toward her. But the philosopher took the girl's hand and said, kindly:—"You must come with me now, my child, and pretend that you know nothing of Caesar's intentions toward you. It is the only way to save you. But while you are with the emperor, who, in any case, can devote but a short time to you to-day, I will return here and consult with your people. There is much to be decided, of the greatest moment, and not to you alone." Melissa turned with tearful eyes to Euryale, and questioned her with a look; whereupon the lady drew the girl's hand out of that of the philosopher, and saying to him, "She shall be with you directly," took her away to her own apartment.

Here she begged Melissa to dry her eyes, and arranging the girl's hair and robe with her own hands, she promised to do all in her power to facilitate her flight. She must do her part now by going into Caesar's presence as frankly as she had done yesterday and the day before. She might be quite easy; her interests were being faithfully watched over.

Taking a short leave of her father, who was looking very sulky because nobody seemed to care for his opinion, and of Alexander, who lovingly promised her his help, she took the philosopher's hand and walked with him through one crowded apartment after another. They often had difficulty in pressing through the throng of people who were waiting for an audience, and in the antechamber, where the Aurelians had had to pay so bitterly for their insolence yesterday, they were detained by the blonde and red-Haired giants of the Uermanian body-guard, whose leader, Sabinus, a Thracian of exceptional height and strength, was acquainted with the philosopher.

Caracalla had given orders that no one was to be admitted till the negotiations with the Parthian ambassadors, which had begun an hour ago, were brought to a conclusion. Philostratus well knew that the emperor would interrupt the most important business if Melissa were announced, but there was much that he would have the maiden lay to heart before he led her to the monarch; while she wished for nothing so earnestly as that the door which separated her from her terrible wooer might remain closed to the end of time. When the chamberlain Adventus looked out from the imperial apartments, she begged him to give her a little time before announcing her.

The old man blinked consent with his dim eyes, but the philosopher took care that Melissa should not be left to herself and the terrors of her heart. He employed all the eloquence at his command to make her comprehend what it meant to be an empress and the consort of the ruler of the world. In flaming colors he painted to her the good she might do in such a position, and the tears she might wipe away. Then he reminded her of the healing and soothing influence she had over Caracalla, and that this influence came doubtless from the gods, since it passed the bounds of nature and acted so beneficently. No one might reject such a gift from the immortals merely to gratify an ordinary passion. The youth whose love she must give up would be able to comfort himself with the thought that many others had had much worse to bear, and he would find no difficulty in getting a substitute, though not so beautiful a one. On the other hand, she was the only one among millions whose heart, obedient to a heaven-sent impulse, had turned in pity toward Caracalla. If she fled, she would deprive the emperor of the only being on whose love he felt he had some claim. If she listened to the wooing of her noble lover, she would be able to tame this ungovernable being and soothe his fury, and would gain in return for a sacrifice such as many had made before her, the blissful consciousness of having rendered an inestimable service to the whole world. For by her means and her love, the imperial tyrant would be transformed into a beneficent ruler. The blessing of the thousands whom she could protect and save would make the hardest task sweet and endurable.

Here Philostratus paused, and gazed inquiringly at her; but she only shook her head gently, and answered:

"My brain is so confused that I can scarcely hear even, but I feel that your words are well meant and wise. What you put before me would certainly be worth considering if there were anything left for me to consider about. I have promised myself to another, who is more to me than all the world—more than the gratitude and blessings of endangered lives of which I know nothing. I am but a poor girl who only asks to be happy. Neither gods nor men expect more of me than that I should do my duty toward those whom I love. And, then, who can say for certain that I should succeed in persuading Caesar to carry out my desires, whatever they might be?"

"We were witnesses of the power you exercised over him," replied the philosopher; but Melissa shook her head, and continued eagerly: "No, no! he only values in me the hand that eases his pain and want of sleep. The love which he may feel for me makes him neither gentler nor better. Only an hour or two before he declared that his heart was inclined to me, he had Titianus murdered!"

"One word from you," the philosopher assured her, "and it would never have happened. As empress, they will obey you as much as him. Truly, child, it is no small thing to sit, like the gods, far above the rest of mankind."

"No, no!" cried Melissa, shuddering. "Those heights! Only to think of them makes everything spin round me. Only one who is free from such giddiness dare to occupy such a place. Every one must desire to do what he can do best. I could be a good housewife to Diodoros, but I should be a bad empress. I was not born to greatness. And, besides—what is happiness? I only felt happy when I did what was my duty, in peace and quiet. Were I empress, fear would never leave me for a moment. Oh. I know enough of the hideous terror which this awful being creates around him; and before I would consent to let it torture me to death by day and by night-morning, noon, and evening—far rather would I die this very day. Therefore, I have no choice. I must flee from Caesar's sight—away hence—far, far, away!"

Tears nearly choked her voice, but she struggled bravely against them. Philostratus, however, did not fail to observe it, and gazed, first mournfully into her face and then thoughtfully on the ground. At length he spoke with a slight sigh:

"We gather experience in life, and yet, however old we may be, we act contrary to it. Now I have to pay for it. And yet it still lies in your hands to make me bless the day on which I spoke on your behalf. Could you but succeed in rising to real greatness of soul, girl—through you, I swear it, the subjects of this mighty kingdom would be saved from great tribulations!"

"But, my lord," Melissa broke in, "who would ask such lofty things of a lowly maiden? My mother taught me to be kind and helpful to others in the house, to my friends, and fellow-citizens; my own heart tells me to be faithful to my betrothed. But I care not greatly for the Romans, and what to me are Gauls, Dacians, or whatever else these barbarians may be called?"

"And yet," said Philostratus, "you offered a sacrifice for the foreign tyrant."

"Because his pain excited my compassion," rejoined Melissa, blushing.

"And would you have done the same for any masterless black slave, covered with pitiably deep wounds?" asked the philosopher.

"No," she answered, quickly; "him I would have helped with my own hand. When I can do without their aid, I do not appeal to the gods. And then— I said before, his trouble seemed doubly great because it contrasted so sharply with all the splendor and joy that surrounded him."

"Aye," said the philosopher, earnestly, "and a small thing that affects the ruler recoils tenfold—a thousand-fold-on his subjects. Look at one tree through a cut glass with many facets, and it be comes a forest. Thus the merest trifle, when it affects the emperor, becomes important for the millions over whom he rules. Caracalla's vexation entails evil on thousands—his anger is death and ruin. I fear me, girl, your flight will bring down heavy misfortune on those who surround Caesar, and first of all upon the Alexandrians, to whom you belong, and against whom he already bears a grudge. You once said your native city was dear to you."

"So it is," returned Melissa, who, at his last words had grown first red and then pale; "but Caesar can not surely be so narrow-minded as to punish a whole great city for what the poor daughter of a gem-cutter has done."

"You are thinking of my Achilles," answered the philosopher. "But I only transferred what I saw of good in Caracalla to the figure of my hero. Besides, you know that Caesar is not himself when he is in wrath. Has not experience taught me that no reasons are strong enough to convince a loving woman's heart? Once more I entreat you, stay here! Reject not the splendid gift which the gods offer you, that trouble may not come upon your city as it did on hapless Troy, all for a woman's sake.

"What says the proverb? 'Zeus hearkens not to lovers' vows'; but I say that to renounce love in order to make others happy, is greater and harder than to hold fast to it when it is menaced."

These words reminded her of many a lesson of Andreas, and went to her heart. In her mind's eye she saw Caracalla, after hearing of her flight, set his lions on Philostratus, and then, foaming with rage, give orders to drag her father and brothers, Polybius and his son, to the place of execution, like Titianus. And Philostratus perceived what was going on in her mind, and with the exhortation, "Remember how many persons' weal or woe lies in your hands!" he rose and began a conversation with the Thracian commander of the Germanic guard.

Melissa remained alone upon the divan. The picture changed before her, and she saw herself in costly purple raiment, glittering with jewels, and seated by the emperor's side in a golden chariot. A thousand voices shouted to her, and beside her stood a horn of plenty, running over with golden solidi and crimson roses, and it never grew empty, however much she took from it. Her heart was moved; and when, in the crowd which her lively imagination had conjured up before her, she caught sight of the wife of the blacksmith Herophilus, who had been thrown into prison through an accusation from Zminis, she turned to Caracalla whom she still imagined seated beside her, and cried, "Pardon!" and Caracalla nodded a gracious consent, and the next moment Herophilus's wife lay on her liberated husband's breast, while the broken fetters still clanked upon his wrists. Their children were there, too, and stretched up their arms to their parents, offering their happy lips first to them and then to Melissa.

How beautiful it all was, and how it cheered her compassionate heart!

And this, said the newly awakened, meditative spirit within her, need be no dream; no, it lay in her power to impart this happiness to herself and many others, day by day, until the end.

Then she felt that she must arise and cry to her friend, "I will follow your counsel and remain! "But her imagination had already begun to work again, and showed her the widow of Titianus, as she entreated Caesar to spare her noble, innocent husband, while he mercilessly repulsed her. And it flashed through her mind that her petitions might share the same fate, when at that moment the emperor's threatening voice sounded from the adjoining room.

How hateful its strident tones were to her ear! She dropped her eyes and caught sight of a dark stain on the snow-white plumage of the doves in the mosaic pavement at her feet.

That was a last trace of the blood of the young tribune, which the attendants had been unable to remove. And this indelible mark of the crime which she had witnessed brought the image of the wounded Aurelius before her: just as he now lay, shaken with fever, so had she seen her lover a few days before. His pale face rose before her inward sight; would it not be to him a worse blow than that from the stone, when he should learn that she had broken her faith to him in order to gain power and greatness, and to protect others, who were strangers to her, from the fury of the tyrant?

His heart had been hers from childhood's hour, and it would bleed and break if she were false to the vows in which he placed his faith. And even if he succeeded at last in recovering from the wound she must deal him, his peace and happiness would be destroyed for many a long day. How could she have doubted for a moment where her real duty lay?

If she followed Philostratus's advice—if she acceded to Caracalla's wishes—Diodoros would have every right to condemn and curse her. And could she then feel so entirely blameless? A voice within her instantly said no; for there had been moments in which her pity had grown so strong that she felt more warmly toward the sick Caesar than was justifiable. She could not deny it, for she could not without a blush have described to her lover what she felt when that mysterious, inexplicable power had drawn her to the emperor.

And now the conviction rapidly grew strong in her that she must not only preserve her lover from further trouble, but strive to make good to him her past errors. The idea of renouncing her love in order to intercede for others, most likely in vain, and lighten their lot by sacrificing herself for strangers, while rendering her own and her lover's life miserable, now seemed to her unnatural, criminal, impossible; and with a sigh of relief she remembered her promise to Andreas. Now she could once more look freely into the grave and earnest face of him who had ever guided her in the right way.

This alone was right—this she would do!

But after the first quick step toward Philostratus, she stood still, once more hesitating. The saying about the fulfilling of the time recurred to her as she thought of the Christian, and she said to herself that the critical moment which comes in every life was before her now. The weal or woe of her whole future depended on the answer she should give to Philostratus. The thought struck terror to her heart, but only for a moment. Then she drew herself up proudly, and, as she approached her friend, felt with joy that she had chosen the better part; yea, that it would cost her but little to lay down her life for it.

Though apparently absorbed in his conversation with the Thracian, Philostratus had not ceased to observe the girl, and his knowledge of human nature showed him quickly to what decision she had come. Firmly persuaded that he had won her over to Caracalla's side, he had left her to her own reflections. He was certain that the seed he had sown in her mind would take root; she could now clearly picture to herself what pleasures she would enjoy as empress, and from what she could preserve others. For she was shrewd and capable of reasoning, and above all—and from this he hoped the most— she was but a woman. But just because she was a woman he could not be surprised at her disappointing him in his expectations. For the sake of Caracalla and those who surrounded him he would have wished it to be otherwise; but he had become too fond of her, and had too good a heart, not to be distressed at the thought of seeing her fettered to the unbridled young tyrant.

Before she could address him, he took his leave of the Thracian. Then, as he led her back to the divan, he whispered: "Well, I have gained one more experience. The next time I leave a woman to come to a decision, I shall anticipate from the first that she will come to an opposite conclusion to that which, as a philosopher and logical thinker, I should expect of her. You are determined to keep faith with your betrothed and stab the heart of this highest of all wooers—after death he will be ranked among the gods—for such will be the effect of your flight."

Melissa nodded gayly, and rejoined, "The blunt weapon that I carry would surely not cost Caesar his life, even if he were no future immortal."

"Scarcely," answered Philostratus; "but what he may suffer through you will drive him to turn his own all-too-sharp sword against others. Caracalla being a man, my calculations regarding him have generally proved right. You will see how firmly I believe in them in this case, when I tell you that I have already taken advantage of a letter brought by the messengers of the empress-mother to take my leave of the emperor. For, I reasoned, if Melissa listens to the emperor, she will need no other confederate than the boy Eros; if, however, she takes flight—then woe betide those who are within range of the tyrant's arm, and ten times woe to me who brought the fugitive before his notice! Early to-morrow, before Caracalla leaves his couch, I shall return with the messengers to Julia; my place in the ship—"

"O my lord," interrupted Melissa, in consternation, "if you, my kind protector, forsake me, to whom shall I look for help?"

"You will not require it if you carry out your intentions," said the philosopher. "Throughout this day you will doubtless need me; and let me impress upon you once more to behave before Caracalla in such a manner that even his suspicious mind may not guess what you intend to do. To- day you will still find me ready to help you. But, hark! That is Caesar raging again. It is thus he loves to dismiss ambassadors, when he wishes they should clearly understand that their conditions are not agreeable to him. And one word more: When a man has grown gray, it is doubly soothing to his heart that a lovely maiden should so frankly regret the parting. I was ever a friend of your amiable sex, and even to this day Eros is sometimes not unfavorably inclined to me. But you, the more charming you are, the more deeply do I regret that I may not be more to you than an old and friendly mentor. But pity at first kept love from speaking, and then the old truth that every woman's heart may be won save that which already belongs to another."

The elderly admirer of the fair sex spoke these words in such a pleasant, regretful tone that Melissa gave him an affectionate glance from her large, bright eyes, and answered, archly: "Had Eros shown Philostratus the way to Melissa instead of Diodoros, Philostratus might now be occupying the place in this heart which belongs to the son of Polybius, and which must always be his in spite of Caesar!"

CHAPTER XXIV.

The door of the tablinum flew open, and through it streamed the Parthian ambassadors, seven stately personages, wearing the gorgeous costume of their country, and followed by an interpreter and several scribes. Melissa noticed how one of them, a young warrior with a fair beard framing his finely molded, heroic face, and thick, curling locks escaping from beneath his tiara, grasped the hilt of his sword in his sinewy hand, and how his neighbor, a cautious, elderly man, was endeavoring to calm him.

Scarcely had they left the antechamber than Adventus called Melissa and Philostratus to the emperor. Caracalla was seated on a raised throne of gold and ivory, with bright scarlet cushions. As on the preceding day, he was magnificently dressed, and wore a laurel wreath on his head. The lion, who lay chained beside the throne, stirred as he caught sight of the new-comers, which caused Caracalla to exclaim to Melissa: "You have stayed away from me so long that my 'Sword of Persia' fails to recognize you. Were it not more to my taste to show you how dear you are to me, I could be angry with you, coy bird that you are!"

As Melissa bent respectfully before him, he gazed delighted into her glowing face, saying, as he turned half to her and half to Philostratus: "How she blushes! She is ashamed that, though I could get no sleep during the night, and was tortured by an indescribable restlessness, she refused to obey my call, although she very well knows that the one remedy for her sleepless friend lies in her beautiful little hand. Hush, hush! The high-priest has told me that you did not sleep beneath the same roof as I. But that only turned my thoughts in the right direction. Child, child!—See now, Philostratus—the red rose has become a white one. And how timid she is! Not that it offends me, far from it—it delights me. —Those flowers, Philostratus! Take them, Melissa; they add less to your beauty than you to theirs." He seized the splendid roses he had ordered for her early that morning and fastened the finest in her girdle himself. She did not forbid him, and stammered a few low words of thanks.

How his face glowed! His eyes rested in ecstatic delight upon his chosen one. In this past night, after he had called for her and waited in vain with feverish longing for her coming, it had dawned on him with convincing force that this gentle child had awakened a new, intense passion in him. He loved her, and he was glad of it—he who till now had taken but a passing pleasure in beautiful women. Longing for her till it became torture, he swore to himself to make her his, and share his all with her, even to the purple.

It was not his habit to hesitate, and at daybreak he had sent for his mother's messengers that they might inform her of his resolve. No one dared to gainsay him, and he expected it least of all from her whom he designed to raise so high. But she felt utterly estranged from him, and would gladly have told him to his face what she felt.

Still, it was absolutely necessary that she should restrain herself and endure his insufferable endearments, and even force herself to speak. And yet her tongue seemed tied, and it was only by the utmost effort of her will that she could bring herself to express her astonishment at his rapid return to health.

"It is like magic," she concluded, and he heartily agreed. Attacks of that kind generally left their effects for four days or more. But the most astonishing thing was that in spite of being in the best of health, he was suffering from the gravest illness in the world. "I have fallen a victim to the fever of love, my Philostratus," he cried, with a tender glance at Melissa.

"Nay, Caesar," interrupted the philosopher, "love is not a disease, but rather not loving."

"Prove this new assertion," laughed the emperor; and the philosopher rejoined, with a meaning look at the maiden, "If love is born in the eyes, then those who do not love are blind."

"But," answered Caracalla, gayly, "they say that love comes not only from what delights the eye, but the soul and the mind as well."

"And have not the mind and the spirit eyes also?" was the reply, to which the emperor heartily assented.

Then he turned to Melissa, and asked with gentle reproach why she, who had proved herself so ready of wit yesterday, should be so reserved today; but she excused her taciturnity on the score of the violent emotions that had stormed in upon her since the morning.

Her voice broke at the end of this explanation, and Caracalla, concluding that it was the thought of the grandeur that awaited her through his favor which confused her and brought the delicate color to her cheeks, seized her hand, and, obedient to an impulse of his better nature, said:

"I understand you, child. Things are befalling you that would make a stouter heart tremble. You have only heard hints of what must effect such a decisive change in your future life. You know how I feel toward you. I acknowledged to you yesterday what you already knew without words. We both feel the mysterious power that draws us to one another. We belong to each other. In the future, neither time nor space nor any other thing may part us. Where I am there you must be also. You shall be my equal in every respect. Every honor paid to me shall be offered to you likewise. I have shown the malcontents what they have to expect. The fate which awaits the consul

Claudius Vindex and his nephew, who by their want of respect to you offended me, will teach the others to have a care."

"O my lord, that aged man!" cried Melissa, clasping her hands, imploringly.

"He shall die, and his nephew," was the inexorable answer. "During my conference with my mother's messengers they had the presumption to raise objections against you and the ardent desire of my heart in a manner which came very near to being treason. And they must suffer for it."

"You would punish them for my sake?" exclaimed Melissa. "But I forgive them willingly. Grant them pardon! I beg, I entreat you."

"Impossible! Unless I make an example, it will be long before the slanderous tongues would hold their peace. Their sentence stands."

But Melissa would not be appeased. With passionate eagerness she entreated the emperor to grant a pardon, but he cut her short with the request not to interfere in matters which he alone had to decide and answer for.

"I owe it to you as well as to myself," he continued, "to remove every obstacle from the path. Were I to spare Vindex, they would never again believe in my strength of purpose. He shall die, and his nephew with him! To raise a structure without first securing a solid foundation would be an act of rashness and folly. Besides, I undertake nothing without consulting the omens. The horoscope which the priest of this temple has drawn up for you only confirms me in my purpose. The examination of the sacrifices this morning was favorable. It now only remains to be seen what the stars say to my resolve. I had not yet taken it when I last questioned the fortune-tellers of the sky. This night we shall learn what future the planets promise to our union. From the signs on yonder tablet it is scarcely possible that their answer should be otherwise than favorable. But even should they warn me of misfortune at your side, I could not let you go now. It is too late for that. I should merely take advantage of the warning, and continue with redoubled severity to sweep away every obstacle that threatens our union. And one thing more—"

But he did not finish, for Epagathos here reminded him of the deputation of Alexandrian citizens who had come to speak about the games in the Circus. They had been waiting several hours, and had still many arrangements to make.

"Did they send you to me?" inquired Caracalla, with irritation, and the freedman answering in the affirmative, he cried: "The princes who wait in my antechamber do not stir until their turn comes. These tradesmen's senses are confused by the dazzle of their gold! Tell them they shall be called when we find time to attend to them."

"The head of the night-watch too is waiting," said the freedman; and to the emperor's question whether he had seen him, and if he had anything of consequence to report, the other replied that the man was much disquieted, but seemed to be exercising proper severity. He ventured to remind his master of the saying that the Alexandrians must have 'Panem et circenses'; they did not trouble themselves much about anything else. In these days, when there had been neither games, nor pageants, nor distribution of corn, the Romans and Caesar had been their sole subjects of conversation. However, there was to be something quite unusually grand in the Circus to-night. That would distract the attention of the impudent slanderers. The night-watchman greatly desired to speak to the emperor himself, to prepare him for the fact that excitement ran higher in the Circus here than even in Rome. In spite of every precaution, he would not be able to keep the rabble in the upper rows quiet.

"Nor need they be," broke in the emperor; "the louder they shout the better; and I fancy they will see things which will be worth shouting for. I have no time to see the man. Let him thoroughly realize that he is answerable for any real breach of order."

He signed to Epagathos to retire, but Melissa went nearer to Caesar and begged him gently not to let the worthy citizens wait any longer on her account.

At this Caracalla frowned ominously, and cried: "For the second time, let me ask you not to interfere in matters that do not concern you! If any one dares to order me—" Here he stopped short, for, as Melissa drew back from him frightened, he was conscious of having betrayed that even love was not strong enough to make him control himself. He was angry with himself, and with a great effort he went on, more quietly:

"When I give an order, my child, there often lies much behind it of which I alone know. Those who force themselves upon Caesar, as these citizens do, must learn to have patience. And you—if you would fill the position to which I intend to raise you—must first take care to leave all paltry considerations and doubts behind you. However, all that will come of itself. Softness and mercy melt on the throne like ice before the sun. You will soon learn to scorn this tribe of beggars who come whining round us. If I flew in a passion just now, it was partly your fault. I had a right to expect that you would be more eager to hear me out than to shorten the time of waiting for these miserable merchants."

With this his voice grew rough again, but as she raised her eyes to him and cried beseechingly, "O, my lord!" he continued, more gently:

"There was not much more to be said. You shall be mine. Should the stars confirm their first revelations, I shall raise you to-morrow to my side, here in the city of Alexandria, and make the people do homage to you as their empress. The priest of Alexandria is ready to conduct the marriage ceremonial. Philostratus will inform my mother of my determination."

Melissa had listened to these arrangements with growing distress; her breath came fast, and she was incapable of uttering a word; but Caesar was delighted at the lovely confusion painted on her features, and cried, in joyful excitement:

"How I have looked forward to this moment—and I have succeeded in surprising her! This is what makes imperial power divine; by one wave of the hand it can raise the lowest to the highest place!"

With this he drew Melissa toward him, kissed the trembling girl upon the brow, and continued, in delighted tones:

"Time does not stand still, and only a few hours separate us from the accomplishment of our desires. Let us lend them wings. We resolved yesterday to show one another what we could do as singers and lute- players. There lies my lyre—give it me, Philostratus. I know what I shall begin with."

The philosopher brought and tuned the instrument; but Melissa had some difficulty in keeping back her tears. Caracalla's kiss burned like a brand of infamy on her brow. A nameless, torturing restlessness had come over her, and she wished she could dash the lyre to the ground, when Caracalla began to play, and called out to Philostratus:

"As you are leaving us to-morrow, I will sing the song which you honored with a place in your heroic tale."

He turned to Melissa, and, as she owned to having read the work of the philosopher, he went on "You know, then, that I was the model for his Achilles. The departed spirit of the hero is enjoying in the island of Leuke, in the Pontus, the rest which he so richly deserves, after a life full of heroic deeds. Now he finds time to sing to the lyre, and Philostratus put the following verses—but they are mine—into his mouth.—I am about to play, Adventus! Open the door!"

The freedman obeyed, and the emperor peered into the antechamber to see for himself who was waiting there.

He required an audience when he sang. The Circus had accustomed him to louder applause than his beloved and one skilled musician could award him. At last he swept the strings, and began singing in a well-trained tenor, whose sharp, hard quality, however, offended the girl's critical ear, the song to the echo on the shores of Pontus:

Echo, by the rolling waters
Bathing Pontus' rocky shore,
Wake, and answer to the lyre
Swept by my inspired hand!

Wake, and raise thy voice in numbers
Sing to Homer, to the bard
Who has given life immortal
To the heroes of his lay.

He it was from death who snatched me;
He who gave Patroclus life;
Rescued, in perennial glory,
Godlike Ajax from the dead!

His the lute to whose sweet accents,
Ilion owes undying fame,
And the triumph and the praises
Which surround her deathless name.

The "Sword of Persia" seemed peculiarly affected by his master's song, which he accompanied by a long-drawn howl of woe; and, before the imperial virtuoso had concluded, a discordant cry sounded for a short time from the street, in imitation of the squeaking of young pigs. It arose from the crowd who were waiting round the Serapeum to see Caesar drive to the Circus; and Caracalla must have noticed it, for, when it waxed louder, he gave a sidelong glance toward the place from which it came, and an ominous frown gathered upon his brow.

But it soon vanished, for scarcely had he finished when stormy shouts of applause rose from the antechamber. They proceeded from the friends of Caesar, and the deep voices of the Germanic bodyguard, who, joining in with the cries they had learned in the Circus, lent such impetuous force to the applause, as even to satisfy this artist in the purple.

Therefore, when Philostratus spoke words of praise, and Melissa thanked him with a blush, he answered with a smile: "There is something frank and untrammeled in their manner of expressing their feelings outside. Forced applause sounds differently. There must be something in my singing that carries the hearers away. My Alexandrian hosts, however, are overready to show me what they think. It did not escape me, and I shall add it to the rest."

Then he invited Melissa to make a return for his song by singing Sappho's Ode to Aphrodite. Pale, and as if obeying some strange compulsion, she seated herself at the instrument, and the prelude sounded clear and tuneful from her skillful fingers.

"Beautiful! Worthy of Mesomedes!" cried Caracalla, but Melissa could not sing, for at the first note her voice was broken by stormy sobs.

"The power of the goddess whom she meant to extol!" said Philostratus, pointing to her; and the tearful, beseeching look with which she met the emperor's gaze while she begged him in low tones—"Not now! I can not do it to-day!"—confirmed Caracalla in his opinion that the passion he had awakened in the maiden was in no way inferior to his own-perhaps even greater. He relieved his full heart by whispering to Melissa a passionate, "I love you," and, desiring to show her by a favor how kindly he felt toward her, added: "I will not let your fellow-citizens wait outside any longer—Adventus! The deputation from the Circus!"

The chamberlain withdrew at once, and the emperor throwing himself back on the throne, continued, with a sigh:

"I wonder how any of these rich tradesmen would like to undertake what I have already gone through this day. First, the bath; then, while I rested, Macrinus's report; after that, the inspection of the sacrifices; then a review of the troops, with a gracious word to every one. Scarcely returned, I had to receive the ambassadors from my mother, and then came the troublesome affair with Vindex. Then the dispatches from Rome arrived, the letters to be examined, and each one to be decided on and signed. Finally the settling of accounts with the idiologos, who, as high-priest of my choosing, has to collect the tribute from all the temples in Egypt. . . . Next I gave audience to several people—to your father among the rest. He is strange, but a thorough man, and a true Macedonian of the old stock. He repelled both greeting and presents, but he longed to be revenged—heavily and bloodily—on Zminis, who denounced him and brought him to the galleys. . . . How the old fellow must have raged and stormed when he was a prisoner! I treated the droll old gray-beard like my father. The giant pleases me, and what skillful fingers he has on his powerful hands! He gave me that ring with the portraits of Castor and Pollux."

"My brothers were the models," remarked Melissa, glad to find something to say without dissembling.

Caracalla examined the stone in the gold ring more closely, and exclaimed in admiration: "How delicate the little heads are! At the first glance one recognizes the hand of the happily gifted artist. Your father's is one of the noblest and most refined of the arts. If I can raise a statue to a lute-player, I can do so to a gem-cutter."

Here the deputation for the arrangement of the festival was announced, but the emperor, calling out once more, "Let them wait," continued:

"You are a handsome race—the men powerful, the women as lovely as Aphrodite. That is as it should be! My father before me took the wisest and fairest woman to wife. You are the fairest—the wisest?—well, that too, perhaps. Time will show. But Aphrodite never has a high forehead, and, according to Philostratus, beauty and wisdom are hostile sisters with you women."

"Exceptions," interposed the philosopher, as he pointed to Melissa, "prove the rule."

"Describe her in that manner to my mother," said Caracalla. "I would not let you go from me, were you not the only person who knows Melissa. I may trust in your eloquence to represent her as she deserves. And now," he continued, hurriedly, "one thing more. As soon as the deputation is dismissed and I have received a few other persons, the feast is to begin. You would perhaps be entertained at it. However, it will be better to introduce you to my 'friends' after the marriage ceremony. After dark, to make up for it, there is the Circus, to which you will, of course, accompany me."

"Oh, my lord!" exclaimed the maiden, frightened and unwilling. But Caracalla cried, decisively: "No refusal, I must beg! I imagine that I have proved sufficiently that I know how to shield you from what is not fitting for a maiden. What I ask of you now is but the first step on the new path of honor that awaits you as future empress."

Melissa raised both voice and hands in entreaty, but in vain. Caracalla cut her short, saying in authoritative tones:

"I have arranged everything. You will go to the Circus. Not alone with me—that would give welcome work to scandalous tongues. Your father shall accompany you—your brothers, too, if you wish it. I shall not join you till after the performance has begun. Your fellow-citizens will divine the meaning of this visit. Besides, Theocritus and the rest have orders to acquaint the people with the distinction that awaits you and the Alexandrians. But why so pale? Your cheeks will regain their color in the Circus. I know I am right— you will leave it delighted and enthralled. You have only to learn for the first time how the acclamations of tens of thousands take hold upon the heart and intoxicate the senses. Courage, courage, Macedonian maiden! Everything grand and unexpected, even unforeseen happiness, is alarming and bewildering. But we become accustomed even to the impossible. A strong spirit like yours soon gets over anything of the kind. But the time is running on. One word more: You must be in the Circus by sunset. In any case, you must be in your place before I come. Adventus will see that you have a chariot or a litter, whichever you please. Theocritus will be waiting at the entrance to lead you to your seats."

Melissa could restrain herself no longer, and, carried away by the wild conflict of passions in her breast, she threw control and prudence to the winds, and cried:

"I will not!" Then throwing back her head as if to call the heavens to witness, she raised her great, wide-open eyes and gazed above.

But not for long. Her bold defiance had roused Caesar's utmost fury, and he broke out with a growl of rage:

"You will not, you say? And you think, unreasoning fool, that this settles the matter?"

He uttered a wild laugh, pressed his hand firmly on his left eyelid, which began to twitch convulsively, and went on in a lower but defiantly contemptuous tone:

"I know better! You shall! And you will not only go to the Circus, but you will do it willingly, or at least with smiling lips. You will start at sunset! At the time appointed I shall find you in your place. If not!—Must I begin so soon to teach you that I can be serious? Have a care, girl! You are dear to me; yet— by the head of my father!—if you defy me, my Numidian lion-keepers shall drag you to the place you belong to!"

Thus far Melissa had listened to the emperor's raging with panting bosom and quivering nostrils, as at a performance, which must sooner or later come to an end; and now she broke in regardless of the consequences:

"Send for them," she cried, "and order them to throw me to the wild beasts! It will doubtless be a welcome surprise to the lookers-on. Which of them can say they have ever seen the daughter of a free Roman citizen who never yet came before the law, torn to pieces in the sand of the arena? They delight in anything new! Yes, murder me, as you did Plautilla, although I never offended either you or your mother! Better die a hundred deaths than parade my dishonor before the eyes of the multitude in the open Circus!"

She ceased, incapable of further resistance, threw herself weeping on the divan, and buried her face in the cushions.

Confounded and bewildered by such audacity, the emperor had heard her out. The soul of a hero dwelt in the frail body of this maiden! Majestic as all-conquering Venus she had resisted him for the second tune, and now how touching did she appear in her tears and weakness! He loved her, and his heart yearned to raise her in his arms, to beg her forgiveness, and fulfill her every wish. But he was a man and a monarch, and his desire to show Melissa to the people in the Circus as his chosen bride had become a fixed resolve during the past sleepless night. And indeed he was incapable of renouncing any wish or a plan, even if he felt inclined to do so. Yet he heartily regretted having stormed at the gentle Greek girl like some wild barbarian, and thus himself thrown obstacles in the way of attaining his desire. His hot blood had carried him away again. Surely some demon led him so often into excesses which he afterward repented of. This time the fiend had been strong in him, and he must use every gentle persuasion he knew of to bend the deeply offended maiden to his will.

He was relieved not to meet her intense gaze as he advanced toward her and took Philostratus's place, who whispered to her to control herself and not bring death and ruin upon them all.

"I Truly I meant well toward you, dearest," he began, in altered tones. "But we are both like overfull vessels—one drop will make them overflow. You—confess now that you forgot yourself. And I—On the throne we grow unaccustomed to opposition. It is fortunate that the flame of my anger dies out so quickly. But it lies with you to prevent it from ever breaking out; for I should always endeavor to fulfill a kindly expressed wish, if it were possible. This time, however, I must insist—"

Melissa turned toward the emperor, and stretching out beseeching hands, she cried:

"Bid me do anything, however hard, and it shall be done, but do not force me to go with you to the Circus. If my mother were only alive! Wherever I could go with her was right. But my father, not to speak of my madcap brother Alexander, do not know what befits a maiden, nor does anybody expect it of them."

"And rightly," interposed Caracalla. "Now I understand your opposition, and thank you for it. But it fortunately lies in my power to remove your objection. The women have to obey me, too. I shall at once issue the necessary orders. You shall appear in the Circus surrounded by the noblest matrons of the city. The wives of these citizens shall accompany you. Even my mother will be sure to approve of this arrangement. Farewell, then, till we meet again in the Circus!"

He spoke the last words with proud satisfaction, and with the grave demeanor that Cilo had taught him to adopt in the curia.

He then gave the order to admit the Alexandrian citizens, and the words of entreaty died upon the lips of the unfortunate imperial bride, for the folding doors were thrown open and the deputation advanced through them.

Old Adventus signed to Melissa, and with drooping head she followed him through the rooms and corridors that led to the apartments of the highpriest.

CHAPTER XXV.

Melissa had wept her fill on the breast of the lady Euryale, who listened to her woes with motherly sympathy, and yet she felt as if a biting frost had broken and destroyed the blossoms which only yesterday had so richly and hopefully decked her young heart. Diodoros's love had been to her like the fair and sunny summer days that turn the sour, hard fruit into sweet and juicy grapes. And now the frost had nipped them. The whole future, and everything round her, now looked gray, colorless, and flat. Only two thoughts held possession of her mind: on the one hand, that of her betrothed, from whom this visit to the Circus threatened to separate her forever; and on the other, that of her imperial lover, to escape whom she would have flown anywhere, even to the grave.

Euryale remarked with concern how weary and broken Melissa looked—so different from her usual bright self, while she listened to her father and Alexander as they consulted with the lady as to the future. Philostratus, who had promised his advice, did not appear; and to the gem-cutter, no proposal could seem so unwelcome as that of leaving his native city and his sick favorite, Philip.

He considered it senseless, and a result of the thoroughly wrong-headed views of sentimental women, to reject the monarch of the world when he made honorable proposals to an unpretending girl. But the lady Euryale — of whom his late wife had always spoken with the highest respect—and, supported by her, his son Alexander, had both represented to him so forcibly that a union with the emperor would render Melissa most unhappy, if it did not lead to death, that he had been reduced to silence. Only, when they spoke of the necessity of flight, he burst out again, declaring that the time had not yet come for such extreme measures.

When Melissa now rejoined them, he spoke of the emperor's behavior toward her as being worthy of a man of honor, and endeavored to touch her heart by representing what an old man must feel who should be forced to leave the house where his father and grandfather had lived before him, and even the town whose earth held all that was dearest to him.

Here the tears which so easily rose to his eyes began to flow, and, seeing that Melissa's tender heart was moved by his sorrow, he gained confidence, and reproached his daughter for having kindled Caracalla's love, by her radiant eyes—so like her mother's! Honestly believing that his affection was returned, Caesar was offering her the highest honor in his power; if she fled from him, he would have every right to complain of having been basely deceived, and to call her a heartless wanton.

Alexander now came to his sister's aid, and reminded him how Melissa had hazarded life and liberty to save him and her brothers. She had been forced to look so kindly into the tyrant's face if only to sue for their pardon, and it became him ill to make this a reproach to his daughter.

Melissa nodded gratefully to her brother, but Heron remained firm in his assertion that to think of flight would be foolish, or at least premature.

At this, Alexander repeated to him that Melissa had whispered in his ear that she would rather die at once than live in splendor, but in perpetual fear, by the side of an unloved husband; whereupon Heron began to breathe hard, as he always did before an outburst of anger.

But a message, calling him to the emperor's presence, soon calmed him.

At parting, he kissed Melissa, and murmured "Would you really drive your old father out of our dear home, away from his work, and his birds—from his garden, and your mother's grave? Is it then so terrible to live as empress, in splendor and honor? I am going to Caesar—you can not hinder me from greeting him kindly from you?"

Without waiting for an answer, he left the room; but when he was outside he took care to glance at himself in the mirror, arrange his beard and hair, and place his gigantic form in a few of the dignified attitudes he intended to adopt in the presence of the emperor.

Meanwhile Melissa had thrown off the indifference into which she had fallen, and her old doubts raised their warning heads with renewed force.

Alexander swore to be her faithful ally; Euryale once more assured her of her assistance; and yet, more especially when she was moved with pity for her father, who was to leave all he loved for her sake, she felt as if she were being driven hither and thither, in some frail bark, at the mercy of the waves.

Suddenly a new idea flashed through her mind. She rose quickly.

"I will go to Diodoros," she cried, "and tell him all! He shall decide."

"Just now?" asked Euryale, startled. "You would certainly not find your betrothed alone, and since all the world knows of Caracalla's intentions, and gazes curiously after you, your visit would instantly be reported to Caesar. Nor is it advisable for you to present yourself before your offended lover, when you have neither Andreas nor any one else to speak for you and take your part."

Melissa burst into tears, but the matron drew her to her and continued tenderly:

"You must give that up—but, Alexander, do you go to your friend, and be your sister's mouthpiece!"

The artist consented with all the ardor of brotherly affection, and having received from Melissa, whose courage began to rise again, strict injunctions as to what he was to say to her lover, he departed on his errand.

Wholly absorbed by the stormy emotions of her heart, the maiden had forgotten time and every external consideration; but the lady Euryale was thoughtful for her, and now led her to her chamber to have her hair dressed for the Circus. The matron carefully avoided, for the present, all mention of her young friend's flight, though her mind was constantly occupied with it— and not in vain.

The skillful waiting-woman, whom she had bought from the house of the priest of Alexander, who was a Roman knight, loosened the girl's abundant brown hair, and, with loud cries of admiration, declared it would be easy to dress such locks in the most approved style of fashion. She then laid the curling-irons on the dish of coals which stood on a slender tripod, and was about to twist it into ringlets; but Melissa, who had never resorted to such arts, refused to permit it. The slave assured her, however, as earnestly as if it were a matter of the highest importance, that it was impossible to arrange the curls of a lady of distinction without the irons. Euryale, too, begged Melissa to allow it, as nothing would make her so conspicuous in her overdressed surroundings as excessive simplicity. That was quite true, but it made the girl realize so vividly what was before her, that she covered her face with her hands and sobbed out:

"To be exposed to the gaze of the whole city—to its envy and its scorn!"

The matron's warning inquiry, what had become of her favorite's high-minded calm, and her advice to restrain her weeping, lest she should appear before the public in the Amphitheater with tear-stained eyes, helped her to compose herself.

The tire-woman had not finished her work when Alexander returned, and Melissa dared not turn her head for fear of disturbing her in her task. But when Alexander began his report with the exclamation, "Who knows what foolish gossip has driven him to this?" she sprang up, regardless of the slave's warning cry. And as her brother went on to relate how Diodoros had left the Serapeum, in spite of the physician's entreaty to wait at least until next morning, but that Melissa need not take it greatly to heart, it was too much for the girl who had already that day gone through such severe and varied experiences. The ground seemed to heave beneath her feet; sick and giddy she put out her hand to find some support, that she might not sink on her knees; in so doing, she caught the tall tripod which held the dish of coals. It swayed and fell clattering to the ground, bringing the irons with it. Its burning contents fell partly on the floor and partly on the festal robe which Melissa had thrown over a chair before loosening her hair. Alexander caught her just in time to prevent her falling.

With her healthy nature, Melissa soon regained consciousness, and during the first few moments her distress over the spoiled garment threw every other thought into the background. Shaking her head gravely over the black-edged holes which the coals had burned in the peplos and the under- robes, Euryale secretly rejoiced at the accident. She remembered that when her heart was torn and bleeding, after the death of her only child, her thoughts were taken off herself by the necessary duty of providing mourning garments for herself, her husband, and the slaves. This trivial task had at least helped her to forget for a few hours the bitterness of her grief.

Only anxious to lighten in some sort the fate of the sweet young creature whom she had learned to love, she made much of the difficulty of procuring a fresh dress for Melissa, though she was perfectly aware that her sister-in-law possessed many such. Alexander was commissioned to take one of the emperor's chariots—which always stood ready for the use of the courtiers between the Serapeum and the springs on the east—and to hasten to the lady Berenike. The lady begged that he, as an artist, would assist in choosing the robe; and the less conspicuous and costly it was the better.

To this Melissa heartily agreed, and, after Alexander had gone, Euryale bore off her pale young charge to the eating-room, where she forced her to take some old wine and a little food, which she would not touch before. As the attendant filled the wine-cup, the high-priest himself joined them, greeted Melissa briefly and with measured courtesy, and begged his wife to follow him for a moment into the tablinum.

The attendant, a slave who had grown gray in the service of Timotheus, now begged the young guest, as though he represented his mistress, to take a little food, and not to sip so timidly from the winecup. But the lonely repast was soon ended, and Melissa, strengthened and refreshed, withdrew to the sleeping-apartment. Only light curtains hung at the doors of the high-priest's hurriedly furnished rooms, and no one noticed Melissa's entrance into the adjoining chamber.

She had never played the eavesdropper, but she had neither the presence of mind to withdraw, nor could she avoid hearing that her own name was mentioned.

It was the lady who spoke, and her husband answered in excited tones:

"As to your Christianity, and whatever there may be in it that is offensive to me as high-priest of a heathen god, we will speak of that later. It is not a question now of a difference of opinion, but of a serious danger, which you with your easily-moved heart will bring down upon yourself and me. The gem-cutter's daughter is a lovely creature— I will not deny it—and worthy of your sympathy; besides which, you, as a woman, can not bear to see her most sacred feelings wounded."

"And would you let your hands he idle in your lap," interposed his wife, "if you saw a lovable, innocent child on the edge of a precipice, and felt yourself strong enough to save her from falling? You can not have asked yourself what would be the fate of a girl like Melissa if she were Caracalla's wife."

"Indeed I have," Timotheus assured her gravely, "and nothing would please me better than that the maiden should succeed in escaping that fate. But — the time is short, and I must be brief—the emperor is our guest, and honors me with boundless confidence. Just now he disclosed to me his determination to make Melissa his wife, and I was forced to approve it. Thus he looks to me to carry out his wishes; and if the maiden escapes, and there falls on you, or, through you, on me, the shadow of a suspicion of having assisted in her flight, he will have every right to regard me as a traitor and to treat me as such. To others my life is made sacred by my high office, but the man to whom a human life—no matter whose—is no more than that of a sacrificial animal is to you or me, that man would shed the blood of us both without a quiver of the eyelid."

"Then let him!" cried Euryale, hotly. "My bereaved and worn-out life is but a small price to pay for that of an innocent, blameless creature, glowing with youth and all the happiness of requited love, and with a right to the highest joys that life can offer."

"And I?" exclaimed Timotheus, angrily. "What am I to you since the death of our child? For the sake of the first person that came to you as a poor substitute for our lost daughter, you are ready to go to your death, and to drag me with you into the gloom of Hades. There speaks the Christian! Even that gentle philosopher on the throne, Marcus Aurelius, was disgusted at your fellow-believers' hideous mania for death. The Christian expects in the next world all that is denied to him in this. But we think of this life, in which the Deity has placed us. To me life is the highest blessing, and yours is dearer to me than my own. Therefore I say, firmly and decidedly: Melissa must not make her escape from this house. If she is determined to fly this night, let her do so—I shall not hinder her. If your counsel is of service to her, I am glad; but she must not enter this house again after the performance in the Circus, unless she be firmly resolved to become Caesar's wife. If she can not bring herself to this, the apartments which belong to us must be closed against her, as against a dangerous foe."

"And whither can she go?" asked Euryale, sadly and with tearful eyes, for there was no gainsaying so definite an order from her lord and master. "The moment she is missed, they will search her father's house; and, if she takes advantage of Berenike's ship, it will soon be discovered that it was your brother's wife who helped her to escape from Caracalla."

"Berenike will know what to do," answered Timotheus, composedly. "She, if any one, knows how to take care of herself. She has the protection of her influential brother-in-law, Coeranus; and just now there is nothing she would not do to strike a blow at her hated enemy."

"How sorrow and revenge have worked upon that strange woman!" exclaimed the lady, sadly. "Caracalla has injured her, it is true—"

"He has, and to-day he has added a further, deeper insult, for he forces her to appear in the Amphitheater, with the wives of the other citizens who bear the cost of this performance. I was there, and heard him say to Seleukus, who was acting as spokesman, that he counted on seeing his wife, of whom he had heard so much, in her appointed place this evening.

"This will add fuel to the fire of her hatred. If she only does not allow her anger to carry her away, and to show it in a manner that she will afterward regret!—But my time is short. I have to walk before the sacred images in full ceremonial vestments, and accompanied by the priest of Alexander. You, unfortunately, take no pleasure in such spectacles. Once more, then—if the girl is determined to fly, she must not return here. I repeat, if any one can help her to get away, it is Berenike. Our sister-in-law must take the consequences. Caesar can not accuse her of treason, at any rate, and her interference in the matter will clear us of all suspicion of complicity."

No word of this conversation had escaped Melissa. She learned nothing new from it, but it affected her deeply.

Warm-hearted as she was, she fully realized the debt of gratitude she owed to the lady Euryale; and she could not blame the high-priest, whom prudence certainly compelled to close his doors against her. And yet she was wounded by his words. She had struggled so hard in these last days to banish all thought of her own happiness, and shield her dear ones from harm, that such selfishness appeared doubly cruel to her. Did it not seem as if this priest of the great Deity to whom she had been taught to pray, cared little what became of his nearest relatives, so long as he and his wife were unmolested? That was the opposite of what Andreas had praised as the highest duty, the last time she had walked with him to the ferry; and since then Johanna had told her the story of Christ's sufferings, and she understood the fervor with which the freedman had spoken of the crucified Son of God—the great example of all unselfishness.

In the enthusiasm of her warm young heart she felt that what she had heard of the Christians' teacher was beautiful, and that she too would not find it hard to die for those she loved.

With drooping head Euryale re-entered the room, and gazed with kind, anxious eyes into the girl's face, as if asking her forgiveness. Following the impulse of her candid heart, Melissa threw her fair young arms round the aged lady, and, to her great surprise, after kissing her warmly on brow and mouth and eyes, cried in tones of tender entreaty:

"Forgive me. I did not want to listen, and yet I could not choose but hear. No word of your discourse escaped me. I know now that I must not fly, and that I must bear whatever fate the gods may send me. I used often to say to myself, 'Of how little importance is my life or my happiness!' And now that I must give up my lover, come what may I care not what the future has in store for me. I can never forget Diodoros; and, when I think that everything is at an end between us, it is as if my heart were torn in pieces. But I have found out, in these last days, what heavy troubles one may bear without breaking down. If my flight is to bring danger, if not death and ruin, upon so many good people, I had better stay. The man who lusts after me—it is true, when I think of his embrace my blood runs cold! But perhaps I shall be able to endure even that. And then—if I crush my heart into silence, and renounce Diodoros forever, and give myself up to Caesar—as I must—tell me you will not then close your doors against me, but that I may stay with you till the horrid hour comes when Caracalla calls me?"

The matron had listened with deep emotion to Melissa's victory over her desires and her aversions. This heathen maiden, brought up in the right way by a good mother, and to whom life had taught many a hard lesson, was she not already treading in the footsteps of the Saviour? This child was offering up the great and pure love of her heart to preserve others from sorrow and danger; and what a different course of action was she herself to pursue in obedience to her husband's orders—her husband, whose duty it was to offer a shining example to the whole heathen world!

She thought of Abraham's sacrifice, and wondered if the Lord might not perhaps be satisfied with Melissa's willingness to lay her love upon the altar. In any case, whatever she, Euryale, could do to save her from the worst fate that could befall a woman, that should be done, and this time it was she who drew the other toward her and kissed her.

Her heart was full to overflowing, and yet she did not forget to warn Melissa to be careful, when she was about to lay her head with its artificially arranged curls upon the lady's breast.

"No, no," she said, tenderly warding off the maiden's embrace. Then, laying her hands on the girl's shoulders, she looked her straight in the face, and continued: "Here you will ever find a resting-place. When your hair lies smoothly round your sweet face, as it did yesterday, then lay it on my breast as often as you will. Aye, and it can and shall be here in the Serapeum; though not in these rooms, which my lord and master closes against you. I told you of the time being fulfilled for each one of us, and when yours came you proved yourself to be the good tree of which our Lord speaks as bearing good fruit. You look at me inquiringly; how indeed should you understand the words of a Christian? But I shall find time enough in the next few days to explain them to you; for—I say it again—you shall remain near me while the emperor searches the city and half the world over for you. Keep that firmly in your mind and let it help to give you courage in the Circus."

"But my father?" cried Melissa, pointing to the curtain, through which Heron's loud voice now became audible.

"Depend on me," whispered the lady, hurriedly; "and rest assured that he will be warned in time. Do not betray my promise. If we were to take him into our confidence now, he would spoil all. As soon as he is gone, and your brother has returned, you two shall hear—"

They were interrupted by the steward, who, with a peculiar smile upon his clean-shaven lips, came to announce Heron's visit.

The communicative gem-cutter had already confided to the servant what it was that agitated him so greatly, but Melissa was astonished at the change in her father's manner.

The shuffling gait of the gigantic, unwieldy man, who had grown gray stooping over his work, had gained a certain majestic dignity. His cheeks glowed, and the gray eyes, which had long since acquired a fixed look from straining over the gemcutting, now beamed with a blissful radiance. Something wonderful must have happened to him, and, without waiting to be questioned by the lady, he poured out to her the news that he would have been overjoyed to have shouted in the market-place for all to hear.

The reception accorded to him at Caesar's table, he declared, had been flattering beyond all words. The godlike monarch had treated him more considerately, nay, sometimes with more reverence, than his own sons. The best dishes had been put before him, and Caracalla had asked all sorts of questions about his future consort, and, on hearing that Melissa had sent him greetings, he had raised himself and drunk to him as if he were a friend.

His table-companions, too, had treated Heron with every distinction. Immediately on his arrival the monarch had desired them to honor him as the father of the future empress. They had all agreed with him in demanding that Zminis the Egyptian should be punished with death, and had even encouraged him to give the reins to his righteous anger. He, if any one, was in the habit of being moderate in all things, if only as a good example to his sons; and he had proved in many a Dionysiac feast that the god could not easily overpower him. The amount of wine he had drunk to-day would generally have had no more effect upon him than water, and yet he had felt now and then as if he were drunken, and the whole festal hall turned round with him. Even now he would be quite incapable of walking forward in a given straight line.

With the exclamation, "Such is life!—a few hours ago on the rowing- bench, and fighting with the brander of the galleys for trying to brand me with the slave-mark, and now one of the greatest among the great!" he closed his tale, for a glance through the window showed him that time pressed.

With strange bashfulness he then gazed at a ring upon his right hand, and said hesitatingly that his own modesty made the avowal difficult to him; but the fact was, he was not the same man as when he last left the ladies. By the grace of the emperor he had been made a praetorian. Caesar had at first wanted to make him a knight; but he esteemed his Macedonian descent higher than that class, to which too many freed slaves belonged for his taste. This he had frankly acknowledged, and the emperor must have considered his objections valid, for he immediately spoke a few words to the prefect Macrinus, and then told the others to greet him as senator with the rank of praetorian.

Then indeed he felt as if the seat beneath him were transformed into a wild steed carrying him away, through sea and sky-wherever it pleased. He had had to hold tightly to the arm of the couch, and only remembered that some one—who it was he did not know—had whispered to him to thank Caesar.

"This," continued the gem-cutter, "restored me so far to myself that I could express my gratitude to your future husband, my child. I am only the second Egyptian who has entered the senate. Coeranus was the only one before me. What favor! And how can I describe what followed? All the distinguished members of the senate and the past consuls offered me a brotherly embrace as their new colleague. When Caesar commanded me to appear at your side in the Circus, wearing the white toga with the broad purple stripe, and I remarked that the shops of the better clothes- sellers would be shut by this time on account of the performance, and that such a toga was not to be obtained, there was a great laugh over the Alexandrian love of amusement. From all sides they offered me what I required; but I gave the preference to Theocritus, on account of his height. What is long enough for him will not be too short for me.—And now one of the emperor's chariots is waiting for me. If only Alexander were at home! The house ought to have been illuminated and hung with garlands for my arrival, and a crowd of slaves waiting to kiss my hands.

"There will soon be more than our two. I hope Argutis may understand how to fasten on the shoes with the straps and the crescent! Philip knows even less of these things than I do myself, besides which the poor boy is laid low. It is lucky that I remembered him. I had very nearly forgotten his existence. Ah!—if your mother were still alive! She had clever-fingers! She—Ah, lady Euryale, Melissa has perhaps told you about her. Olympias she was called, like the mother of the great Alexander, and, like her, she bore good children. You yourself were praising my boys just now. And the girl! . . Only a few days ago, it was a pretty, shy thing that no one would ever have expected to do anything great; and now, what have we not to thank that gentle child for? The little one was always her mother's darling. Eternal gods! I dare not think of it! If only she who is gone might have had the joy of hearing me called senator and praetor! O child! if she could have sat with us to-day in the emperor's seats, and we two could have seen you there—you, our pride, honored by the whole city, Caesar's future bride."

Here the strong man with the soft heart broke down, and, clasping his hands over his face, sobbed aloud, while Melissa clung to him and stroked his bearded cheeks.

Under her loving words of consolation he soon regained his composure, and, still struggling against the rising tears, he cried:

"Thank Heaven, there can be no more foolish talk of flight! I shall stay here; I shall never take advantage of the ivory chair that belongs to me in the curia in Rome. Your husband, my child, and the state, would scarcely expect it of me. If, however, Caesar presents me as his father, with estates and treasures, my first thought shall be to raise a monument to your mother. You shall see! A monument, I tell you, without a rival. It shall represent the strength of man submissive to womanly charm."

He bent down to kiss his daughter's brow, and whispered in her ear:

"Gaze confidently into the future, my girl. A father's eye is not easily deceived, and so I tell you—that the emperor has been forced to shed blood do insure the safety of the throne; but, in personal intercourse with him, I learned to know your future husband as a noble-hearted man. Indeed, I am not rich enough to thank the gods for such a son-in-law!"

Melissa gazed after her father, incapable of speaking. It went to her heart that all these hopes should be changed to sorrow and disappointment through her. And so she said, with tearful eyes, and shook hey head when the lady assured her that with her it was a question of a cruelly spoiled life, whereas her father would only have to renounce some idle vanities which he would forget as easily as he had seized upon them.

"You do not know him," answered the maiden, sadly. "If I fly, then he too must hide himself in a far country. He will never be happy again if they take him from the little house—his birds—our mother's grave. It was for her sake alone that he took no thought for the ivory seat in the curia. If you only knew how he clings to everything that reminds him of our mother, and she never left our city."

Here she was interrupted by the entrance of Philostratus. He was not alone; an imperial slave accompanied him, bringing a graceful basket with gifts from the emperor to Melissa.

First came a wreath of roses and lotos-flowers, looking as if they had been plucked just before sunrise, for among the blossoms and leaves there flashed and sparkled a glittering dew of diamonds, lightly fastened on delicate silver wires. Next came a bunch of flowers, round whose stems a supple golden snake was twined, covered with rubies and diamonds and destined to coil itself round a woman's arm. The third was a necklace of extremely costly Persian pearls, which had once belonged—so the merchant had declared—to great Cleopatra's treasure.

Melissa loved flowers; and the costly gifts that accompanied them could not fail to rejoice a woman's heart. And yet she only gave them a passing glance, reddening painfully as she did so.

What the bearer had to say to her was of more importance to her than the gifts he brought, and in fact the troubled manner of the usually composed philosopher betrayed that he had something more serious to deliver than the gifts of his love-sick lord.

The lady Euryale, perceiving that he meant to try once more to persuade Melissa to yield, hastened to declare that she had found ways and means to help the maiden to escape; but he shook his head with a sigh, and said, thoughtfully:

"Well—well—I shall go on board the ship while the wild beasts are doing their part in the Circus. May we meet again happily, either here or else where! My way leads me first to Caesar's mother, to inform her of his choice of a wife. Not that he needs her consent: whose consent or disapproval does Caracalla care for? But I am to win Julia's heart for you. Possibly I may succeed; but you—you scorn it, and fly from her son. And yet—believe me, child—the heart of that woman is a treasure that has no equal, and, if she should open her arms to you, there would be little that you could not endure. When I left you, just now, I put myself in your place, and approved of your resolve; but it would be wrong not to remind you once more of what you must expect if you follow your own will, and if Caesar considers himself scorned, ill-treated, and deceived by you."

"In the name of all the gods, what has happened?" broke in Melissa, pallid with fear. Philostratus pressed his hand to his brow, and his voice was hoarse with suppressed emotion as he continued: "Nothing new- only things are taking their old course. You know that Caracalla threatened old Claudius Vindex and his nephew with death because of their opposition to his union with you. We all hoped, however, that he would be moved to exercise mercy. He is in love—he was so gracious at the feast! I myself was foremost among those who did their utmost to dispose Caesar to clemency.. But he would not be moved, and, before the sun goes down upon this day, the old man and the young one—the chiefest among the nobles of Rome—will be no more. And it is Caracalla's love for you, child, that sheds this blood. Ask yourself after this how many lives will be sacrificed when your flight causes hatred and fury to reign supreme in the soul of the cheated monarch!"

With quickened breath Euryale had listened to the philosopher, without regarding the girl; but scarcely had Philostratus uttered his last words than Melissa ran to her, and, clasping her hands passionately on the matron's arm, she cried, "Ought I to obey you, Euryale, and the terrors of my own heart, and flee?"

Then releasing the lady, she turned again to the philosopher, and burst out: "Or are you in the right, Philostratus? Must I stay, to prevent the misery that threatens to overtake others?"

Beside herself, torn by the storm that raged in her soul, she clasped her hands upon her brow and continued, wildly: "You are both of you so wise, and surely wish the best. How can you give me such opposite advice? And my own heart?—why have the gods struck it dumb? Time was when it spoke loudly enough if ever I was in doubt. One thing I know for certain: if by the sacrifice of my life I could undo it all, I would joyfully cast myself before the lions and panthers, like the Christian maiden whom my mother saw smiling radiantly as she was led into the arena. Splendor and power are as hateful to me as the flowers yonder with their false dew. I was ever taught to close my ear to the voice of selfishness. If I have any wish for myself, it is that I may keep my faith with him to whom it was promised. But for love of my father, and if I could be certain of saving many from death and misery, I would stay, though I should despise myself and be separated forever from my beloved!"

"Submit to the inevitable," interposed the philosopher, with eager entreaty. "The immortal gods will reward you with the blessings of hundreds whom a word from you will have saved from ruin and destruction."

"And what say you?" asked the maiden, gazing with anxious expectancy into the matron's face. "Follow your own heart!" replied the lady, deeply moved.

Melissa had hearkened to both counselors with eager ear, and both hung anxiously on her lips, while, as if taken out of herself, she gazed with panting bosom into the empty air. They had not long to wait. Suddenly the maiden approached Philostratus and said with a firmness and decision that astonished her friend:

"This will I do—this—I feel it here—this is the right. I remain,
I renounce the love of my heart, and accept what Fate has laid upon me.
It will be hard, and the sacrifice that I offer is great. But I must
first have the certainty that it shall not be in vain."

"But, child," cried Philostratus, "who can look into the future, and answer for what is still to come?"

"Who?" asked Melissa, undaunted. "He alone in whose hand lies my future. To Caesar himself I leave the decision. Go you to him now and speak for me. Bring him greeting from me, and tell him that I, whom he honors with his love, dare to entreat him modestly but earnestly not to punish the aged Claudius Vindex and his nephew for the fault they were guilty of on my account. For my sake would he deign to grant them life—and liberty? Add to this that it is the first proof I have asked of his magnanimity, and clothe it all in such winning words as Peitho can lay upon your eloquent lips. If he grants pardon to these unfortunate ones, it shall be a sign to me that I may be permitted to shield others from his wrath. If he refuses, and they are put to death, then will he himself have decided our fate otherwise, and he sees me for the last time alive in the Circus. Thus shall it be—I have spoken."

The last words came like a stern order, and Philostratus seemed to have some hopes of the emperor's clemency, for his love's sake, and the philosopher's own eloquence. The moment Melissa ceased, he seized her hand and cried, eagerly:

"I will try it; and, if he grant your request, you remain?"

"Yes," answered the maiden, firmly. "Pray Caesar to have mercy, soften his heart as much as you are able. I expect an answer before going to the Circus."

She hurried back into the sleeping-room without regarding Philostratus's answer. Once there, she threw herself upon her knees and prayed, now to the manes of her mother, now—it was for the first time—to the crucified Saviour of the Christians, who had taken upon himself a painful death to bring happiness to others. First she prayed for strength to keep her vow, come what might; and then she prayed for Diodoros, that he might not be made wretched if she found herself compelled to break her troth with him.

Her father and brothers, too, were not forgotten, as she commended their lives to a higher power.

When Euryale looked into the room, she found Melissa still upon her knees, her young frame shaken as with fever. So she withdrew softly, and in the Temple of Serapis, where her husband served as high-priest, she prayed to Jesus Christ that he who suffered little children to come unto him would lead this wandering lamb into the right path.

———————————

Milton Keynes UK
Ingram Content Group UK Ltd.
UKHW010842110324
438959UK00019B/361

9 789357 946599